THE ROMAN MYSTERIES

the
Sewer
Demon

Also by Caroline Lawrence

THE ROMAN MYSTERIES

The First Roman Mysteries Quiz Book
The Second Roman Mysteries Quiz Book
Trimalchio's Feast and Other Mini-mysteries
The Legionary from Londinium and Other Mini-mysteries
The Roman Mysteries Treasury
From Ostia to Alexandria with Flavia Gemina

THE P.K. PINKERTON MYSTERIES

The Case of the Deadly Desperados

THE ROMAN MYSTERY SCROLLS

the Sewer Demon

CAROLINE LAWRENCE

Orion
Children's Books

First published in Great Britain in 2012
by Orion Children's Books
a division of the Orion Publishing Group Ltd
Orion House
5 Upper St Martin's Lane
London WC2H 9EA
An Hachette UK company

3 5 7 9 10 8 6 4

A catalogue record for this book is
available from the British Library.

ISBN 978 1 4440 0455 7

Printed in Great Britain by Clays Ltd, St Ives plc

To Dr Gemma Jansen, who generously shared her research on Roman latrines, demons and the goddess Fortuna

SCROLL I

Threptus the Roman beggar boy was usually alert to danger. Years of sleeping rough in the graveyard and scrounging scraps in the market had made him as wary as a fox in the arena.

But on this day – the Nones of November – he was thinking about honey cakes and so he did not notice the three boys following him.

Threptus was eight years old, with tawny hair and bright, hopeful eyes. The boys following him were not much older, but their eyes were cold and hard.

Threptus shifted the heavy palm-leaf basket on his shoulder as he left the Marina Market. He had done well by bartering cheerfully with the stall-keepers. With just the two sesterces entrusted to him by his mentor, he had bought carrots, leeks, apples, white onions and half a dozen sardines. And he still had one coin left. It was a brass dupondius that would buy either half a dozen brown rolls or two honey cakes from Pistor the baker.

It was almost noon. Threptus had not eaten all day and he was famished. Should he spend his last coin on six rolls? Or on the two honey cakes?

At the thought of warm, sweet honey cakes, Threptus's stomach growled hungrily.

He had just passed through the arch of the Marina Gate when a figure suddenly blocked his way and a familiar voice said, 'Where do you think you're going?'

Threptus's empty stomach gave a lurch.

He saw a dirty pair of feet in battered sandals, the grubby calves of bare legs, a ragged brown tunic and a rust-red cloak. Finally he looked up into the sneering face of the town bully. Red-haired Naso could have been good-looking, but his expression made him ugly.

'Well?' said Naso. 'Answer me! Where are you going?'

'Home,' lied Threptus, trying not to let his voice quaver.

Naso sneered. 'You don't have a home,' he said. 'You sleep rough in the graveyard, just like the rest of us. Or have you moved in with that fat chicken-seller?'

Without waiting for an answer, Naso stepped forward and pulled open the basket hanging from Threptus's shoulder. He took out two white onions, and weighed them in each hand.

Then he threw one at a stray dog and bit into the other one. 'Did you get all this food by begging?' he asked, his mouth full.

Threptus glared at him. 'No.'

'Stole it, did you?' said Naso smugly. He hooked his left arm around Threptus's slender neck and brought his face close. The smell of onion was almost overpowering. 'I knew you'd come round to my way of thinking.'

'I didn't steal it,' said Threptus defiantly. 'I'm not a beggar any more. Or a thief.'

'Oh, yeah? Then what are you?' Flecks of half-chewed onion spattered Threptus.

He averted his face. 'I'm an apprentice.'

'Ooh! An apprentice! So you're all high and mighty now. Learning a trade. Who's your master? That fat fake who sells willies on chains and pretends he can see romance in an old lady's future?'

'He's not a fake!' said Threptus angrily. 'I help him and he lets me do the shopping.'

As soon as he said it, he knew he had made a mistake.

'Oh ho!' said Naso. 'That means you must have some money . . . Grab him, boys!'

Threptus felt his arms gripped hard from behind. He didn't have to turn his head to know it was Quartus and Quintus. Once they had been his friends, but now they were in Naso's gang.

Threptus struggled but could not stop Naso from thrusting two fingers roughly into his belt pouch. The older boy groped around for a moment and then pulled out Threptus's last coin.

'Ooh, look!' said Naso, taking a step back. 'It's a dupondius. A bright, shiny dupondius of Domitian. I think I'll keep this to remind me who our new emperor is.'

'No!' Threptus cried, still struggling. 'You can't! It's not yours. That's stealing.'

'It's what we do, me old son!' Naso was only fourteen but he called anybody younger than himself 'me old son'. He slipped the coin into his own belt pouch. 'If you leave that fat crook and join us again, you could go back to stealing, too. Deal?'

Threptus shook his head. He had only been in Naso's gang for two weeks, but he had hated every minute.

'Too bad,' said Naso.

He ripped the basket from Threptus's shoulder and tossed it aside. Apples and carrots tumbled out and rolled across the street. The sardines splatted on the paving stones.

Threptus writhed free and tried to grab some of the apples, but he didn't get far.

Naso kneed him hard in the stomach.

Threptus fell onto his knees, retching and gasping.

He felt the sole of Naso's sandal on his left shoulder and the world was suddenly upside down and his head cracked hard against a paving stone. He saw something like bright gnats flying in front of his vision and he heard the boys laughing.

Then they started to kick him.

SCROLL II

A S THE BULLIES STARTED TO KICK
Threptus, he squinched his eyes shut and
chopped out with his legs and hands. After a
moment his right hand connected with a bony
ankle. Threptus grasped it, tugged hard, and
felt the boy unbalance.

Threptus opened his eyes just in time
to see Quartus fall against Quintus, who

slipped on a sardine and stumbled sideways into Naso.

Fortuna was smiling on Threptus. All three bullies fell backwards into the Hydra fountain in a splashing tangle of arms and legs. This unexpected blessing from the goddess gave Threptus the chance he needed.

He leapt to his feet and ran.

Threptus ran towards the forum, dodging around men in tunics and women in stolas and between a line of naked slaves being led to the auction platform.

He sped past the central notice board and headed towards the place where he had last seen his mentor: the colonnade of the money-changers. A man in a toga was just emerging from this colonnade, head down and counting his money. Threptus almost ran into him, but swerved just in time to avoid a collision. He veered into the colonnade, and ran between columns on his left and the tables of bankers, moneychangers, scribes and will-makers on his right.

Where was his mentor? He usually walked up and down here in the shade, holding up a fistful of amulets, and announcing that they were 'only five sesterces'.

Slowing to a jog, Threptus glanced over his shoulder. Naso and the other two were charging along the colonnade after him, about a hundred paces behind. They were soaking wet and furious.

At last Threptus saw his mentor. Aulus Probus Floridius was a plump Roman citizen with a cheerful grin, an unshaved chin and a grubby tunic. In his wine-spotted toga and tattered garland, he reminded Threptus of Bacchus, the Roman god of wine.

Floridius didn't usually sit at a table, but he was sitting at one now. He had spread out his wares on its surface and he had a good number of customers crowding around. At the moment he was holding up a small bronze charm shaped like a boy's private parts. It was his most popular model and always sold briskly.

Threptus skidded to a stop. How could he tell his master he had nothing to show for the two sesterces he had been given?

'This one is especially good for warding off the evil eye,' Floridius was saying to a woman in a dark blue stola and palla.

Threptus decided not to interrupt his master in the middle of a sale, but he badly needed his protection. He glanced back along the colonnade.

Naso and the other two boys had stopped running but they were still moving towards him through the crowds. Their eyes were fixed on him and they were breathing hard.

'Bk-bk-bk-bk-bk!'

Some of the money-changers and bankers had watchdogs underneath their tables. Floridius was the only one with a chicken. Threptus saw that Floridius's table was a sturdy wooden one and that gave him an idea.

'Brp, brp!' said Aphrodite the hen as Threptus joined her under the table. From under here he could see Floridius's twine-repaired sandals and chubby calves. And the big leather satchel open on his lap.

'Look, boys!' Naso's sneering voice was still breathless. 'He's hiding under the table.'

Threptus peered up at them. He knew they couldn't drag him out and beat him up with all these people around.

'He's chicken,' said Naso.

'He's a big chicken!' said Quintus. 'A big chicken with a little one.'

'Bk-bk-bk-bk-bk!' said Quartus. His mother had dropped him on his head when he was a baby and he liked to imitate animals.

'Bk-bk-bk, b'kak!' said Aphrodite.

'Bk-bk-bk, b'kak!' echoed Quartus.

'Shut up, you idiot,' scowled Naso, and slapped the back of Quartus's head.

'Hey, you boys!' shouted the banker at the table next to Floridius. 'I told you before: I don't want you louts hanging around my stall! Get out of here, or I'll set Fido on you!'

Threptus looked over at Fido. He was a bandy-legged white dog with a jutting lower jaw and a red leather collar. He had been licking his private parts but when he heard his name he jumped to attention and growled.

The banker's name was Dexter. He growled, too. 'Did you hear me? Go on! Get out of here!'

Naso pretended not to hear, but his shoulder twitched and he said, 'Come on, lads.'

But before they left, Naso turned and jabbed the forefinger of his left hand at Threptus, as if to say 'I'll get you!'

'B'kak!' said Aphrodite softly, after the bullies had gone. She was a black, silky chicken and she purred when you stroked her.

Threptus stroked her.

Aphrodite purred.

Floridius's knee nudged Threptus and his cheerful unshaven face appeared upside down. 'Threptus,' he whispered. 'Go keep an eye out for the magistrate! Rufus went home sick and I grabbed his table. I've never done so much business. Ha, ha! Whistle if you see him coming.'

Threptus nodded and scrambled out from under the table.

He quickly glanced around to make sure Naso was gone, then went to the nearest column, hooked an arm around it and stood up on its square base.

From here he could see most of the forum and he could hear his mentor, even above the buzz of voices and clink of coins.

Floridius was making another sale. He had front teeth a bit like a rabbit's and they made him lisp. 'Five sesterces,' he was telling a man in a threadbare grey tunic. 'You can have it for only five sesterces.'

'Don't you have anything cheaper?' asked the man.

'Five sesterces isn't much to pay for wealth and prosperity,' urged Floridius.

Threptus's tummy growled. If his mentor's amulets brought wealth and prosperity, why had they been living on nothing but omelettes made from sacred-chicken eggs?

But maybe their luck had changed. If none of the magistrates appeared, maybe they would have honey cakes yet.

SCROLL III

THREPTUS HAD LIVED IN OSTIA ALL
his life – eight whole years – and he knew
most of the people milling about. But a few
were new to him. As well as looking out for the
magistrate, Threptus decided to hone his skills
of observation by guessing who the strangers
were.

That man with a portable display of sandals

and shoes must be a new cobbler in town. And the muscular youth with the soot-smudged sleeveless tunic and leather satchel full of tools was certainly a travelling blacksmith.

Sometimes a person's scent was a clue. Two slaves who smelt strongly of pee probably worked at a fuller's, where urine was used to bleach clothes. A whiff of horse manure accompanied the stable boy as he strolled past with a tavern serving-girl: she smelt of sour wine. Some people could be identified by sound alone. Threptus closed his eyes for a moment. He could hear Praeco the town crier bellowing that it was a quarter of an hour till noon. Indus the snake-charmer was fluting a cobra up from his basket. He could hear the buzzing whine of the knife-grinder Cultellus. And in the forum school down at the other end of the colonnade, the boys chanted the first lines of an epic poem. In Greek.

Threptus knew that even the colour of a person's clothes could provide a clue about their profession. That man in the black hooded cloak was probably an undertaker. A tunic with two narrow, vertical, red stripes showed that its wearer was an equestrian: a class of Roman rich enough to own a horse. Those shaven-headed men in strapless linen sheaths were priests of Isis.

That stout woman in a leek-green stola and matching parasol looked familiar. Threptus knew she must be rich because she had a slave-girl in attendance. As she passed by, he caught a whiff of her expensive perfume: balsam and rose-oil. Then he remembered. She was the wife of a perfume-maker.

A moment later he heard the woman in leek-green address his mentor.

'Are you the soothsayer?'

'At your service,' lisped Floridius.

'My house is haunted!' she said.

Threptus cocked his head. That sounded interesting.

'Can you get rid of evil spirits?' asked the woman. 'And demons?'

'Of course!' said Floridius. 'That's me specialty! Evil spirits, demons and the evil eye. Ha, ha, ha! How does it manifest?'

This talk of demons was too fascinating to ignore. Threptus moved around his column a little so that he could watch them out of the corner of his eye.

'I hear strange noises in the garden at night. Sometimes in the kitchen, too,' said the woman.

'But have you ever *seen* the demon?'

'Only once. I saw the shadow of something tall and thin in the garden, like a snake but rising straight up into the air. I ran back into my room. Since then I've been too terrified to look.'

'Has your slave-girl seen it?'

The girl shook her head.

'Husband?' asked Floridius.

'My husband died a few months ago. So now it's just me and Zmyrna here.'

'Commiserations!' said Floridius. And then added: 'Could it be your husband's spirit? Was he given the proper rites?'

'Yes,' said the lady. 'We used Ostia's best undertaker.'

'Robber, then? Could a robber be making the noises?'

'We double-bolt the door and the windows are high and barred. Besides, nothing's missing.'

'Could it be some kind of animal? Or a bird?'

The woman shook her head. 'Definitely not.

Last night it knocked over a big amphora in my kitchen.'

Threptus fell a thrill of fear.

'That was why I finally decided to do something about it,' said the woman.

'Have no fear,' said Floridius, 'I shall write you a spell which you must recite. Only five sesterces.'

Her leek-green parasol swayed as she shook her head. 'No. I want someone to come and keep vigil and catch the spirit and cast it out. If you can do that, I will pay you thirty sesterces!'

'Bk-bk-bk, b'kak!' clucked Aphrodite.

'Thirty?' exclaimed Floridius. His jaw dropped but he quickly recovered himself. He sucked his breath through his teeth. 'Ooh, I don't know. Keeping a vigil is dangerous, especially on the night of a full moon. Seventy sesterces.'

'Bk-bk-bk, b'kak!' clucked Aphrodite.

'Why should a full moon matter?' said the woman. 'It will give you light to see. Forty sesterces.'

'Yes, but the full moon also gives demons greater power. Sixty sesterces.'

'Bk-bk-bk, B'KAK!' clucked Aphrodite a third

time, and at the same moment Threptus heard the distinctive clink of hobnailed boots and the cry of, 'Make way for the magistrate. Make way!'

Turning back to the forum, Threptus saw Bacillus the lictor with his ceremonial bundle of sticks. Behind him walked Ostia's duumvir, the most important magistrate of all, Marcus Artorius Bato.

The two of them were heading straight for Floridius and they did not look happy.

Threptus wet his lips, formed his mouth into a tight circle, and blew.

And that was when he remembered.

He had never learned how to whistle.

SCROLL IV

MARCUS ARTORIUS BATO, OSTIA'S
duumvir, was heading straight for
Floridius. Once again, Threptus tried to whistle
a warning to his mentor.

The only result was a faint hissing sound.

Threptus tried a third time, for good luck.

When nothing came, he jumped off the base
of the column and yelled, 'Run, mentor! Run!'

Floridius looked up in alarm. When he saw Bacillus the lictor striding towards him, with Bato the magistrate close behind, his eyes bulged.

'Great Juno's beard!' he exclaimed. With a stroke of his forearm, he swept the amulets and charms off the table and into his open satchel. A heartbeat later he was off and running.

'Bk-bk-bk-bk-bk!' clucked Aphrodite, as if to say, 'What about me?'

Threptus ran to Aphrodite, scooped her up and charged after his mentor. As he passed the lady in leek-green, he accidentally jostled her.

'Stop!' she cried after Floridius. 'You don't know my name or where I live!'

'Stop!' cried the lictor. 'By the order of the duumvir.'

'Stop!' cried Bato. 'You don't have a licence!'

But Floridius and Threptus did not stop.

They pelted along the shaded colonnade, causing Ostians to jump back, merchants to curse and watchdogs to bark. As Threptus ran, Aphrodite cried 'Bk-bk-bk, b'kah!'. He guessed she was telling him not to squeeze her too tightly, so he loosened his grip a little.

At the end of the colonnade Floridius veered left. As he did so, his wobbly buttock gave a banker's table a glancing blow. Silver, brass and copper coins spilled down onto the pavement. They jingled merrily, some even rolling out into the forum. With cries of delight, a dozen Ostians sprang forward, eager to help the banker collect his money. Threptus was agile and managed to dodge around them, but a quick glance over his shoulder showed him that the excited coin-hunters were momentarily blocking Bato's way.

'Bk-bk-bk, b'kak!' clucked Aphrodite excitedly.

Threptus allowed himself a giggle of relief.

But Floridius was stout and already he was slowing down and gasping for breath. Soon Bato and his lictor would catch them up.

'Master!' gasped Threptus. 'We need to find a place to hide.'

'Bk-bk-bk, B'KAK!' clucked Aphrodite the hen, and she pooed with excitement.

That gave Threptus an idea.

'The forica of the Forum Baths!' Threptus called to his mentor. 'The public toilets. We can hide in there!'

'Never been there . . .' gasped Floridius. 'Too posh for me!'

'Don't worry,' said Threptus. 'You don't have to pay to use them. They're free!'

'Not sure . . . where they are!' wheezed Floridius.

'I know the way,' cried Threptus. 'Follow me!'

He sped past Floridius and turned right and then left, hoping that his mentor was following.

'Bk-bk-bk, B'KAK!' cried Aphrodite. She seemed to be telling him to 'Hurry up!'

Threptus put on a burst of speed. He knew Floridius was still behind him; he could hear him wheezing and the slap of his sandals on the paving stones.

'This way!' he cried, and sprinted towards the revolving wooden door that led into Ostia's most opulent public toilets. Sometimes there was a queue to get in, but thankfully not today.

Threptus plunged into the revolving door and pushed with his shoulder.

'Bk-bk-bk-bk-bk!' Aphrodite clucked as she and Threptus emerged into the public latrines.

The large room was dim but colourful, with frescoed walls, a marble floor and vaulted ceiling. It smelt strongly of incense and faintly of poo. Around three walls of the room was a marble bench with a channel of running water at its foot. Eighteen holes on top of the bench were paired with eighteen holes at the front, with a slot cut out between the two holes to make a keyhole shape. These were the toilets. There were no dividing walls and no doors, so Threptus could see half a dozen men sitting over some of the holes, all doing their business.

Threptus quickly scanned the men to see if any of them might pose a threat.

A skinny man in a pale blue tunic was whistling and looking up at the windows, which were high and arched.

A bearded man in a nut-brown tunic was grunting and staring at the diamonds, squares and circles in the coloured marble floor.

A bald man in a yellow tunic was gazing at a fountain. Its jet of softly splashing water masked other sounds and helped cool the room. Somehow a duck had found his way into the latrine and was swimming happily in the fountain.

'Bk-bk-bk, b'kak!' said Aphrodite.

'Quack!' said the duck.

'It wasn't me,' said the bald man in yellow. 'It was the duck what made that noise.'

A fat man in a cream tunic with the two thick, vertical, red stripes of a patrician was gazing at a fresco of Fortuna on the wall opposite. His lips were moving and Threptus guessed he was asking the goddess of luck to keep away evil. Everyone knew that demons lived in the sewers beneath the toilets.

Two muscular men in short, red tunics were sitting next to each other and chatting in low voices. One of them had just leant forward to remove something from a stone bowl full of vinegar at the base of the small fountain.

It was a spongia: a stick the length of Threptus's forearm and thickness of his thumb with a sponge tied at one end. The stick could be easily thrust through the hole at the front of the toilet bench and the damp sponge used to clean the bottom. This way people could wipe themselves efficiently and comfortably, without even standing up. Threptus glanced at the bowl; he knew you did not want to grasp the wrong end of *those* sticks.

The man pushed his spongia through the hole at the front of the bench. A moment later he removed the poo-smeared sponge and dipped it in the channel of running water at his feet. Then he stood up and replaced the sponge-stick in the bowl of vinegar – ready for the next person to use. He nodded goodbye to his friend, stepped into the revolving wooden door and pushed vigorously.

As he exited, Floridius was spun into the latrine.

'Oh dear!' gasped Floridius, his ivy-leaf garland askew. 'Oh dear, oh dear!' He saw the men staring at him and grinned sheepishly. 'Hello,' he said. 'Ha, ha! How is everybody today?'

The bald man in the yellow tunic emitted a rude noise from his bottom.

'May Fortuna aid you in your efforts,' said Floridius politely. Then he saw Threptus. 'Oh, there you are!' he said, and lowered his voice. 'So where's the back door?'

'Back door?' said Threptus.

'I thought that was your plan?'

'No,' Threptus confessed. 'There is no back door.'

'Bk-bk-bk, b'kak!' said Aphrodite.

'But what if they follow us in?' gasped Floridius.

'I don't know,' said Threptus. His throat felt tight. Once again, he had let his mentor down.

Floridius clutched his leather shoulder-bag protectively. 'I was selling without a licence. They could confiscate me charms, amulets and money. Take me to court, too.'

'Bk-bk-bk, b'kah!' Threptus was holding Aphrodite too tightly again.

Threptus looked around. But there was nowhere to hide the bag . . . Unless . . . Threptus beckoned Floridius down to his level, stood on tiptoe and whispered instructions in his mentor's ear.

'But if I do that, then I could lose everything!' lisped Floridius.

'But at least they can't take you to court,' said Threptus.

From outside came the ominous chink of

hobnail boots and the magistrate's voice: 'Where could he have gone?'

The lictor's reply: 'Maybe in there, sir! In the public toilets.'

Threptus and Floridius stared at each other in horror.

Bato and his lictor were right outside.

They were trapped in the poo house!

SCROLL V

THREPTUS WAS SITTING ON ONE OF the shorter end-benches of the marble toilet, holding a sponge-stick and pretending to do his business. He had put Aphrodite the sacred chicken down on the coloured marble floor. She was pecking at something in the channel of water that ran beneath his dangling feet. That channel was where the men rinsed their sponge-sticks; Threptus didn't want to think about what Aphrodite might be eating.

Floridius sat on one of the toilets across the room. He was staring at the ceiling, whistling an innocent tune. He had his hands behind him, and his leather satchel was nowhere in sight.

Threptus looked up at the fresco of Fortuna, smiling down on them all. 'Please, Fortuna,' he prayed. 'Don't let any demons in here. And keep the magistrate out, too.'

Fortuna might be able to stop demons, but she couldn't stop the magistrate.

The revolving door squeaked and Bato appeared in the latrine.

Threptus kept his head down. He hoped Bato wouldn't realise he was with Floridius.

'Evaporatus,' came Bato's ironic voice. 'I thought it was you.'

'Are you talking to me?' said Floridius, pretending to be surprised.

'You know I am,' said Bato.

'Me name isn't Evaporatus.' Floridius gave the magistrate a queasy smile.

'I know,' said Bato icily. 'It's Floridius.'

'Wrong again,' said Floridius, his grey eyes

wide with innocence. 'You've got me mixed up with me brother. His name is Floridius.'

'Are you telling me you're not Floridius the Soothsayer and seller of magic charms who was sitting at Rufus's spot today without either permit or licence?'

'Must have been me brother,' said Floridius.

'Your twin brother, I suppose,' said Bato, his voice heavy with sarcasm.

'Actually,' said Floridius. 'We're triplets. There's me and me brother and me . . . er . . . other brother!'

'Three of you?' said Bato drily. 'What a terrifying prospect. And what's your name?'

'Me name?'

'Your name.'

'Er . . . me name is Aulus Probus . . .' Floridius looked desperately around the forica. 'Spongia!' he announced at last. 'Aulus Probus Spongia!'

'So you're telling me that your name is Sponge-stick?'

'That's right! Exactly right.'

Some of the men in the latrine chuckled. A few others quickly wiped their bottoms and hurried out.

Bato put his hands on his hips. 'Well then, Aulus Probus Spongia . . . What have you got behind your back?'

'Nothing!' said Floridius. 'Nothing at all. Ha, ha!' He laughed nervously, showing his rabbit teeth.

'Show me.'

'Show you what?'

'Show me your hands,' said Bato.

Bacillus the lictor had come in to stand beside Bato, so Threptus had to lean to one side in order to see Floridius. First his mentor held up one chubby hand, then he put it behind his back and held up the other.

'Hold up both hands together,' commanded Bato.

There was a pause and then a gigantic, splashy PLOP!

'Great Jupiter's eyebrows!' exclaimed the lictor. 'What was that?'

Floridius gave an exaggerated shrug and opened his palms to the ceiling to show Bato his hands were empty.

Threptus did not wait to see any more. He was off his seat and into the revolving door.

He knew that the loud plop had been caused by Floridius's leather satchel full of charms, amulets and coins. Threptus knew he had to get it back, or there would be no honey cakes tonight. Maybe not even dinner!

Still holding a spongia, Threptus ran along the sunny street. When people saw him brandishing a bottom-wiper, they leapt back to give him a wide berth.

Threptus turned up a shade-dappled side street and skidded to a stop at a sewer cover near a tall poplar tree. It was a circular marble disc with the face of the river god, Tiber, carved into it. The open mouth, nostrils and eyes served as a drain for rainwater, and received libations of wine during Tiber's feast days.

But the scary-looking sewer cover also had another use.

Demons liked damp, dark sewers. But they did not like images that stared back at them, like actors' masks or Medusa's face. This drain cover with its empty eyes and gaping mouth was apotropaic, designed to scare away demons. Just looking at it made Threptus shiver.

Once or twice in his begging days, Threptus

and his friends had removed this sewer cover and used a small fishing net on a stick to see what they could find. A root of the poplar slowed the flow of water near a bend in the tunnel so that heavy objects like coins and hairpins sometimes collected in a certain spot.

The marble manhole cover was too heavy for Threptus to lift with his fingertips. In the past, he had used a thick twig. Today he had a sturdy lever in the form of his spongia. Using the stick end as a wedge, he was able to pry open the heavy marble disc. Then he sat on the street and used both feet to push it to one side.

As soon as the cover was off, he could hear the gurgling water and smell the sickly sweet odour of sewage.

A few interested bystanders were already gathering around to see what he was up to. Some of them were blocking his light. Even so, he could see that Floridius's leather satchel was not in the bend behind the poplar root. However there *were* a few glints of coins beneath the brown water.

Threptus stretched out on his stomach, then wormed his way forward so that his top half was in the sewer and his hips and legs still outside. If he went any further in he might overbalance.

He stretched out his hand to reach the coins. He could see a tiny copper quadrans, but more importantly a silver denarius! That coin was enough to buy sixteen honey cakes. The mere thought made his mouth water and his tummy growl.

'What do we have here?' came Naso's voice. 'Threptus the beggar boy again! Trying to get into the sewer where he belongs!'

Threptus froze.

Then tried to wiggle back out.

But two pairs of hands had gripped his ankles and were holding him fast.

Threptus was trapped.

'I've heard there are demons down there,' said Naso. 'Demons in the sewers. Have you heard that, boys?'

'Yeah, boss,' came Quintus's voice.

'Hoo-hoo!' said Quartus, imitating an owl.

'Well, most of them just give you the evil eye,' sneered Naso. 'But I've heard there's a big one down there that eats you alive.'

Once again Threptus tried to back out of the sewer. But the boys held him fast.

'That's right,' continued Naso. 'The demon lives in the sewers and it feeds on poo and pee. Sometimes it likes to wait underneath the toilets of the public latrines and when you sit to do your business it pulls you right down! Especially little boys like Threptus.'

'I am not a little boy,' shouted Threptus. 'I am eight years old!'

Naso laughed. 'Well, as you're so big and strong, why don't you go have a look for it? See if you can find the sewer demon. You gave us a dunking. Now it's our turn to give you one!'

Quartus quacked and Threptus felt a sandalled foot rest on his backside. The brothers Quartus and Quintus let go. The foot pushed and . . .

Splash!

Threptus tumbled head first into Ostia's sewer.

SCROLL VI

THREPTUS HAD THE SENSE TO CLOSE
his mouth and eyes before he hit the
water. For a moment he was dazed. Then he
sat up and wiped his eyes with the back of
his arm. The water was only half a foot deep,
so there was no danger of drowning, but he
had hurt his hands putting them out to break
his fall. And he had cracked his head so that

bright gnats swarmed in front of his vision again.

He rubbed his eyes and the gnats faded, but something else was wrong.

It was getting darker by the moment.

He was going blind!

Threptus heard a grinding noise above him and looked up.

With the help of Quartus and Quintus, Naso was replacing the circular manhole, blocking out the bright daylight.

'No!' cried Threptus.

But it was too late. The heavy marble cover settled into place above him with a grinding finality.

'Let me out!' cried Threptus. 'Please!'

He could hear muffled laughter from up above, and Quartus crowing like a rooster, and then angry voices. Were some of the passers-by trying to help?

He waited, hardly daring to breathe, hoping for the cover to come off again.

But it remained in place.

Nobody was coming to help him.

Threptus sat in six inches of smelly, brown

water and tried hard not to cry. He sniffed back tears and took a breath.

'What would Lupus do?' he asked himself.

Lupus was Threptus's hero, an ex-beggar boy who had gone from rags to riches by solving mysteries and helping people.

Threptus touched his talisman – Lupus's wax tablet – hidden down the neck of his tunic. He knew that in a situation like this, Lupus would be brave.

Threptus nodded. 'Be brave,' he told himself. 'Be brave.'

As he looked around, he realised it was not pitch black down here. There were five beams of light coming down from the Tiber drain cover: a big beam from the mouth, two medium beams from the eyes, and two thin beams from the nostrils. As Threptus's eyes adjusted he could see the shape of the sewer. It was a rectangular tunnel, not quite large enough for him to stand upright. He would have to hunch over, like Atlas under the weight of the sky.

That gave him an idea. He stood up so that he was directly beneath the sewer cover. For a moment he listened.

Silence. Had Naso and his gang got bored and wandered off?

Threptus offered up a silent prayer to Father Tiber, whose sewer this was, then put his shoulders to the manhole cover and used both hands to push up.

'Nghhh!'

Nothing.

Threptus took a deep breath and then pushed again, this time with all his might. The manhole cover started to lift. His small biceps bulged. He could do it!

For a moment it was getting brighter, then BAM! He was plunged into darkness again as the manhole cover was stamped back into place.

Threptus could hear Naso's muffled laughter on the street above, and Quartus crowing again.

He knew he was not getting out that way.

He must try to find another exit.

Threptus touched Lupus's wax tablet again and this time he offered up a prayer to Fortuna, the goddess who protected you against sewer demons.

'Be brave, be brave!' he imagined Lupus telling him.

He turned and slowly began to slosh through the dim sewer.

The rectangular tunnel was faced top and bottom and on both sides with stone slabs. Threptus reached out to steady himself, then quickly brought away his hand; the walls were covered with slime, perhaps some kind of moss.

Or something worse.

Beneath his feet was a soft layer; he could feel it squelching through his toes. It was probably mud.

Or something worse.

On the dark surface of the water, something floated by. A small brown log.

Or something worse.

Threptus stood back to let it pass and whispered to himself, 'Be brave, be brave!'

At first the smell almost made him pass out, but he found it was bearable if he breathed through his mouth. He guessed lots of water from the drains of the baths flowed here, diluting the poo and pee. There must be waste water from other places, too. The potters used water to make their clay wet. Also the fullers. But they used urine, too, and that wasn't a good thought. When he caught a whiff of the smelly murex dye used for purple cloth, he knew he must be passing the drain of a dyer's workshop.

It was clammy and cold down here, and he could hear water dripping.

Beams of light shone down from drains above. Some of them were as thin as strands of wool from the spindle. Others were as thick as his forearm. Some drains had square or diamond-shaped holes, caused by the grille above. In a place where a part of the stone-lined wall had cracked to make a ledge, he saw a rat. It glared at him with red eyes, but when he made the sign against evil, it scuttled away.

Presently Threptus came to a place where the sewer divided. After a moment's hesitation, he took the larger right-hand route. A few paces further on, the tunnel was half blocked where the stone facing had fallen down and some earth had spilled out. There were more rats here, but they disappeared into hidden tunnels. Threptus squeezed through the narrow space as quickly as he could. He had heard stories of poisonous water-snakes and toads, too.

And of course there were the demons.

Would he know a demon if he saw one?

One type of demon looked like a goat-bearded man with horns on its head, wings on its back and a giant eye where its belly button should have been. Threptus had seen it scratched into the red plaster wall of the public toilets. He shuddered at the memory.

But he knew that demons could take many shapes. Some demons took the shape of cats and others of owls. You could tell it was a demon if it stared at you. The trick was not to look directly back, lest it give you the evil eye.

And if you *did* look at it, you had to make the sign against evil by stretching forth your left hand, palm forward, and by spitting thrice.

Threptus shuddered, then froze. As if summoned by his fear, something dark and bulky was swimming towards him. It looked like a giant hairless rat.

Threptus spat three times, made the sign against evil with his left hand and covered his eyes with his right. Then he spread the fingers to peek a little. He could not see its face or eyes, but he could see that it was swimming slowly towards him.

Threptus's heart was pounding so hard that the sound of it filled his world.

He knew with terrible certainty that the thing in the water was a sewer demon.

SCROLL VII

AS THE SEWER DEMON SWAM TOWARDS
Threptus, he backed away, stumbled and
found himself sitting on his bottom.

'Ahhh!' he cried, as he shuffled backwards like
a crab.

A moment later the blocked part of the tunnel
stopped his retreat.

His knees were poking up out of the water.

As the sewer demon's hairless, leathery body bumped into them, Threptus squinched his eyes closed, so it could not give him the evil eye, then kicked at it with his feet.

'Ahhh!' he yelled. 'Go away!'

The demon clanked softly and moved away, then drifted against his legs again.

It did not try to bite him or grab him. It felt like a large, leathery bladder ball.

Threptus opened one eye.

The thing bumping against Threptus's legs was not a demon.

Threptus opened his other eye.

It was a leather bag full of clinking things.

Threptus almost sobbed with relief.

It was the satchel full of charms and amulets that his mentor had dropped into the toilet. It was partly filled with air, which had kept it afloat. Its bulk must have slowed it down as the water swirled it along.

Threptus offered up a prayer of thanks and pulled the strap of the satchel over his head and one shoulder. He stood on trembling legs and promptly banged his head on the roof.

'Pollux!' Threptus cursed and rubbed the bump on his head.

Now that his heart was no longer pounding with fear, he could hear something. The sound of faintly echoing men's voices.

He cocked his head and listened, then took a few steps forward, remembering to duck down this time.

Now the sound of gurgling water was added to the muffled voices. Threptus moved cautiously forward and around a slight bend in the sewer. The tunnel was bigger and a little brighter up ahead. There was another sewer cover there! Four leaf-shaped beams of light shone down and reflected off the surface of the tan water, which sloshed around his legs as he waded forward.

The voices came more clearly now and also the splash of running water.

The sewer cover was above him, showing four leaf-shaped glimpses of blue sky. It was square and smaller than the Father Tiber cover, but he was sure he could fit through it. He put his hands against it and found he could lift it easily. Praise Fortuna! But instead of pushing it away he hesitated, then let the square sewer cover settle back into place.

One of the men's voices sounded familiar.

Taking a deep breath, Threptus bravely made his way towards the men's voices and sound of running water. Around another bend in the sewer was an even larger space, where he could stand upright without ducking. He could see water gushing out at the far end. The water smelt of scented oil and made oily bubbles where it hit the sewer water. He guessed this must be the main drain of some public baths. He watched with fascination as various things floated past: a long strung-together clump of hair, a few beauty plasters, an apple core, and some small dark floating things that might have been olives or black beans.

Or something worse.

Then Threptus looked up.

He nearly burst out laughing. Above his head were the naked bottoms of several men, framed by the circles cut in a long marble bench. He was directly underneath the public toilets where he and Floridius had been hiding only a quarter of an hour before! The bottoms were close enough so that he could have reached up and touched them.

He watched in fascination as a sponge-stick came through one of the front holes in the bench to wipe the bottom of the man sitting there. Then the sponge-stick withdrew and the light in the space grew a little brighter as the man stood up.

Threptus was surprised to see that only two of the eighteen holes were now occupied. The empty holes let in a fair amount of light, and he could see quite well down here. And he could hear a familiar voice that made his eyes grow wide.

It was the voice of Marcus Artorius Bato, Ostia's duumvir.

'You don't think they all left because of me, do you?' said Bato's voice.

'You are a bit explosive today, sir,' came the lictor's voice. His must be the bottom next to Bato's.

'I suppose I shouldn't have had that cheese last night,' said Bato. 'Cheese always upsets my stomach.'

Threptus shrank back as Bato's bottom loudly demonstrated the effects of cheese.

'But when Gamala offers,' continued Bato, 'you can't refuse.'

'You were dining with the Pontifex Volcani?' Bacillus sounded surprised.

'Yes,' replied Bato. 'He's a pompous old fool. But his daughter Lucilia is lovely. I've been thinking: perhaps it's time I marry . . . What do you think of her as a possible wife?'

'She'd be quite a trophy, sir. Highborn, beautiful, daughter of the priest of Vulcan . . .'

'And I think she finds me attractive. Urgh!' groaned Bato, as another bottom explosion occurred. 'No more cumin-dusted eggs for me!'

'E UGEPAE!' CRIED FLORIDIUS, WHEN HE
saw Threptus holding out his satchel full
of charms. He stepped through the front door
of his wooden shack, then stopped. 'Pwah!' he
cried. 'You smell like a thousand sponge-sticks!'

'I know,' said Threptus ruefully. 'I spent half
an hour down in the sewers. Should I go to the
baths?'

'Great Juno's beard, no!' cried Floridius. 'Who'd want a dip after you've been in? Best go down to the beach and give yourself a good dunk in the sea.'

'But it's November!' protested Threptus.

'The day is mild,' said Floridius.

'The water is cold,' countered Threptus.

'How do you know?' Floridius narrowed his eyes. 'You never go in.'

'Sometimes I swim in the sea,' said Threptus.

'You can swim?'

Threptus nodded. 'If my feet touch the bottom.'

Floridius chuckled and reached out a hand to ruffle Threptus's hair. He stopped himself just in time and withdrew his hand with a sheepish smile.

'Tell you what,' lisped Floridius. 'Why don't we go down to the beach together? I should wash me charms and amulets. Don't want them smelling of poo, do we? Some of them are probably ruined. But we should be able to save most of them.' He stepped back inside, grabbed a cloak from a peg in the wall, then pulled the squeaky door shut behind him. 'You can tell me how you recovered me satchel on the way.'

As they walked towards the Marina Gate, Threptus told Floridius how Naso had robbed him and later thrown him into the sewers and how he'd thought the satchel was a latrine demon at first and also that he'd overheard the duumvir and his lictor in the public toilets.

'Ooh!' said Floridius. 'Tell me. What did Bato say?'

'He said he had dinner with a "pompous old fool" but he likes the daughter and might marry her.'

'What's her name?'

'Lucilia.'

'Daughter of Gamala?'

'Yes,' said Threptus. 'That was his name.'

'Ah!' said Floridius. 'The Pontifex Volcani, a very important man. You say Bato called Gamala a "pompous old fool"? Hee, hee! Anything else?'

Threptus nodded. 'Cheese and spiced eggs make Bato's poo . . .' He stopped, glanced around, then beckoned Floridius down to his level.

When the soothsayer lowered his shaggy head, Threptus whispered something in his ear.

Floridius recoiled. 'Urgh!' he said. 'That's more than I need to know. Now, come on, let's get you cleaned up!'

They passed beneath the lofty arch of the Marina Gate, skirted the Marina Market and when they found a stretch of deserted beach near the small Temple of the Jews, Threptus ran down through the soft sand to the shore. When he was a few feet from the little waves, he shrugged off the satchel.

'No!' cried Floridius. 'Take me satchel in with you! But don't let any of the charms float away. Or any sesterces.'

Threptus did as he was told.

The sun was still warm but the water was cold.

Threptus stood it for as long as he could, letting the seawater slosh around him and even ducking right under: once, twice and thrice for good luck. He dunked the satchel, too, but was careful not to let any of the charms or coins fall out.

At last he emerged, shivering and dripping

wet. Floridius went to meet him and used his cloak to towel down Threptus. Then the two of them sat on the warm sand by the water, going through the amulets in Floridius's satchel. The ones with feathers or ribbons had to be thrown away, but the bronze and wooden figurines seemed fine. Most of the good luck charms were apotropaic, for turning away evil. In addition to the little bronze willies, Floridius had Medusas, twisted horns, and hands making various gestures. He also had lots of blue-and-white glass disks that looked like eyes.

'How do these keep away evil?' asked Threptus, holding up one of the large flattened blue glass beads.

Although they were alone on the beach, Floridius leaned forward and whispered. 'If a person, demon, lemur or larva gives you the evil eye, then this gives it back.' He smacked his hands together. 'The evil eyes crash together in mid-air. Can't hurt you if you're wearing this.'

Threptus frowned down at a bronze Medusa he was drying with a corner of Floridius's cloak.

'What's a larva?' he asked. 'I thought it was the thing actors wear on their faces.'

'It's also the word for spirit of the dead, because their faces look like what actors wear, only all pale and gauze-like.' Floridius held up a small bronze mask with holes for the eyes and mouth. 'These are the best against larvae,' he said. 'Fight fire with fire.'

'Have you ever seen a larva?'

Floridius nodded. Then he made the sign against evil – his left hand raised palm forward – and spat for extra protection. 'Once I saw one in the woods near the necropolis on mid-summer's eve,' he whispered. 'Larvae are attracted to boundaries and borders. Like where the woods end and the beach starts. Or town walls. Or where the underworld meets our world. That's why they like sewers.'

Threptus made the sign against evil and spat, too.

'That's why they like midnight,' added Floridius. 'And mid-summer. It's where the first half meets the second half.'

Threptus gazed at Floridius with admiration. 'You're so wise,' said Threptus. 'Why don't you always sit at a table in the money-changers' colonnade?'

'Don't have a licence,' said Floridius.

'Why won't they give you a licence?' said Threptus. 'You help people.'

'I do, indeed, little friend,' said Floridius, and sighed. 'The problem is that Bato and I have had dealings before. I once worked in his vineyard out by Laurentum. He doesn't like me. I doubt I'll get a licence as long as he is chief magistrate.' He stared sadly out to sea. 'I just wish I knew that woman's name.'

'What woman?'

'A woman came to see me about exorcising a spirit from her house. She was about to agree to pay me fifty sesterces and dinner, too. But Bato chased me off before I could get her name.'

Threptus's stomach growled fiercely at the mention of dinner. He pressed his hand hard against his stomach. 'I don't know her name,' he said, 'but she smelled of balsam and rose-oil. I think her husband used to make ointments and perfumes. But he died, didn't he?'

'Ha, ha!' Floridius struggled to his feet and

did a little jig on the sand. 'Little friend, you are worth your weight in gold!'

'I am?'

'You are. Think about it. There can't be that many widows of perfume-makers in Ostia. Come on! Let's go find her.'

SCROLL IX

MOST OF OSTIA'S WAREHOUSES AND workshops were close to the River Tiber. Floridius and Threptus began their investigation there. By questioning shop-keepers and passers-by, they soon learned that a perfume-maker called Unguentarius had died during the dog days of August. They found out the name of his widow, too.

Allia Porra lived in a small house in Perfume Alley, behind one of the biggest warehouses on the river.

She herself opened the door and her eyes widened with surprise. 'How did you know where to find me?' she asked. 'I never told you my name.'

'The entrails of me sacred chickens never lie,' declared Floridius with a bow.

Threptus bit his lower lip to keep from smiling. Floridius never killed his chickens. He loved them too much.

'And who is this?' asked Allia Porra, looking down her narrow nose at Threptus.

'This is me apprentice,' lisped Floridius. 'He will be keeping the vigil with me tonight.'

'A mere boy?'

'This is no mere boy,' cried Floridius. 'His mother was a witch from Thrace and his father a priest of Sabazios!' Floridius lifted the palms of both hands, gazed up into the sky and held this dramatic pose. 'He has the Sight!'

Threptus looked at Floridius in surprise, then stood a little taller. He liked the exotic parents Floridius had invented for him.

'Well, I suppose you'd better come in, then,' said Allia Porra.

During his life as a beggar, Threptus had seen the inside of most of Ostia's public buildings, but he had only been in three private houses.

He had been inside Floridius's shack, because that was where he now lived.

He had been inside the house of a rich girl named Pollitta, who lived near Floridius.

And now he was inside the house of the perfume-maker's widow, Allia Porra.

The house had an inner garden, like Pollitta's, but it was only one storey tall, like Floridius's.

'My slave-girl, Zmyrna, should have opened the door,' said Allia. 'But she is sitting on the latrine.'

'You have an indoor latrine?' said Threptus, amazed.

Allia gave him a strange look. 'Of course we do. Doesn't everyone?'

Floridius gently elbowed Threptus in the shoulder. 'We use a chamber pot at our residence,' he said grandly. 'I find it attracts fewer flies.'

'Here's Zmyrna now,' said Allia, as the thin

slave-girl hurried up. 'Come, Zmyrna, let us show the soothsayer and his apprentice the rooms of the house.'

Allia and her slave-girl led the way along a gravel path through a dense and fragrant inner garden. A few quick sniffs told Threptus that thyme, mint, verbena and lavender grew here. A glance showed him rose bushes, jasmine and lilies.

'What's that?' he asked, pointing at a small, spiny grey tree in the centre of the garden. It looked barren and dead amidst the other lush plants.

'Myrrh,' said Allia. 'My husband used its sap for his perfumes. Ugly isn't it?'

'Yes,' said Threptus. He stepped off the path and picked his way through shrubs for a closer look.

'Careful,' said Allia. 'There's a well at the foot of that tree. It's a bit overgrown. I must tell Zmyrna to weed this garden.'

'You have your own well?' asked Threptus. Another step took him closer to the grey tree with its sharp thorns. Near the base of its trunk he could just make out the mouth of the well: a low curving brick wall, half hidden by weeds.

'We don't use the well,' said Allia. 'The water is bad. My husband only used the water for his garden.'

Threptus stepped over a patch of rosemary and leaned forward to look down into the well. He could see the dark glint of water only a few feet below. The sickly sweet whiff of sewage made him recoil. He made his way back to the path and scampered after the others.

On the far side of the garden was a columned walkway with three doors leading to three rooms. From left to right as he faced them were a study, a kitchen and a large bedroom.

Allia showed them the bedroom first. It had black frescoed panels with chubby, winged cupids performing various tasks.

Floridius stepped into the room and began to do a strange thing with his head, rolling it on his chubby neck and intoning: 'Hmmm. Ummm. Bummm.' Then he moved around the room with his head cocked and his eyes half closed and his hands raised.

'What are you doing?' asked Allia.

'Scanning the room for lemures, larvae and/ or demons,' murmured Floridius.

Threptus and the two women watched him for a while. After a moment, Threptus moved forward to examine the cupids on the walls.

'What are they doing?' he asked.

'Making perfume,' said Allia. She came up behind him and pointed. 'See them pressing flowers? And there they are, simmering the petals in brass pans and then straining the essence through muslin into olive oil and then decanting the unguent into jars.'

'Hmmm. Ummm. Bummm,' said Floridius. Threptus saw him open one eye and look at a narrow cot beside a larger bed: 'The gods tell me you that you both sleep in this room!' He announced.

'That's right,' said Allia. 'Since the evil spirit came, Zmyrna has been sleeping in here with me. We bolt the door from the inside after dark.'

Threptus turned away from the cupids. 'Where did Zmyrna sleep before?' he asked. 'Is there another bedroom?'

'When my husband was alive,' said Allia,

'Zmyrna put her cot in the kitchen by the hearth. Come, I'll show you.'

A few moments later, Threptus stood in the kitchen doorway and inhaled. It smelled of beans, cheese and fish sauce, with a faint, sweet undertone of perfume. Along the left-hand wall ran a hearth, with a stone sink and work-table at the near end. Against the right-hand wall, resting on the sandy floor, were a range of large jugs, amphoras and a dolium of water so big that Threptus could have climbed in and been totally submerged. Above these large jars was a shelf of smaller pots and bottles. In the right-hand rear corner of the kitchen – partially screened by a small partition – was a wooden-seated latrine.

'Big kitchen,' said Floridius.

Allia nodded. 'It's big because my husband used to experiment making perfumes and ointments.' She pointed up at bunches of dried herbs and flowers hanging from a beam across the ceiling. 'He used plants and herbs from our garden.'

'Hmmm. Ummm. Bummm,' intoned Floridius as he drifted around the room with his hands up.

Threptus noticed an amphora with a pointed bottom resting in a cone-shaped dent in the sandy kitchen floor. Although it was leaning against the wall, it was almost as tall as he was. His sharp eye noticed letters painted on its shoulder. He went closer and brought his face right up to the letters: GARVM.

'Garv Um?' he read after a while.

'Garum,' corrected Floridius. 'Remember the V can be a U?'

'This big jar is full of garum?' he asked in amazement. He had only tried garum twice in his whole life because it was so expensive.

'It is,' said Allia. 'My husband adored it.'

'So do I.' Threptus's stomach growled fiercely.

Allia gave him a keen look, then smiled.

When Floridius had finished his humming and bumming, Allia led the way out of the kitchen and into the study. The walls in here were painted in coloured panels of blood red and mustard yellow. A tall, bronze standing lamp with a dozen wicks occupied one corner, and a small shrine the other. In the centre of the room was a rectangular wooden table, two wooden chairs, a folding stool and a big leather chair.

'Hmmm. Ummm. Bummm. What? No snake?' Floridius stopped before the small shrine. 'You should have a bronze snake in your lararium to keep away evil. Or at least paint one on.'

'My husband hated snakes,' said Allia. 'But now that he's gone I suppose I could get one.'

'I can get you a bronze one,' said Floridius. 'Very cheap. Only five sesterces. And you should each wear one of me amulets. Here, let me show you.'

He opened a flap on his leather satchel, still damp with seawater, and pulled out his bundle of amulets. As he spread them out on the table, Threptus wandered into the garden again.

He was so hungry that he was tempted to pull up a handful of mint and stuff it into his mouth. There were some chives in one corner and he plucked a few and chewed them, but they only roused his appetite further.

His stomach gave an angry twist and he had to push his hand against it to stop it growling. He looked at the spiky myrrh tree and sighed. Why couldn't it be an apple tree? Or a fig? Or even a lemon tree? What good were thorns when you were hungry?

He went back to the study to find Allia and Zmyrna each putting on new amulets. They had each bought a little bronze Medusa with her snaky hair and staring eyes.

Allia looked up from examining hers. 'These charms are all very well, but can you really get rid of the spirit?'

Floridius nodded and struck an orator's pose with one finger raised. 'Have no fear, Floridius is here!'

'I do hope so,' sighed Allia. She glanced at Threptus, who was still pressing his hand to his stomach. 'Now, it doesn't take a prophet to divine that at least one of you is very hungry. Would you and your apprentice like to join us for dinner?'

T HEY ATE SITTING AT THE WOODEN
table in the study. Once she had put dinner
on the table, the slave-girl, Zmyrna, pulled up a
stool. Threptus was surprised to see her join them.
Once or twice, when peeking through a barred
window into a private house, he had seen slaves
standing attentively near their reclining masters.
Slaves didn't usually dine with their owners.

71

Dinner was a hearty salad made of three different types of beans mixed with cubes of goats' cheese and slices of onion. It was delicious, especially when sprinkled with garum from a square bottle of pale-green glass. It was the best garum Threptus had ever tasted. The dark brown fish sauce was salty and pungent and it made his tongue tingle. He sprinkled some onto his brown rolls, even though there was a saucer of olive oil for dipping the bread.

'You eat garum on bread?' asked Allia, raising an eyebrow.

Threptus nodded happily and tipped the last of the brown liquid onto his third roll.

'Would you like some more?'

'Yes, please!' Threptus nodded enthusiastically.

'Then will you help Zmyrna refill the bottle?'

'Yes,' said Threptus.

Zmyrna took the empty garum bottle and Threptus followed her into the kitchen.

'You hold bottle,' said Zmyrna. 'We mustn't spill. Is very expensive.'

Threptus stared at her. It was the first time he had heard her speak.

Zmyrna went to the amphora marked GARVM and uncorked it. Then she embraced the tall jar in her arms and slowly tipped it down. Threptus held the bottle close to the mouth of the amphora and when the stream of pungent brown liquid suddenly gurgled out, he caught almost all of it. Only a little of the garum overflowed and made a patch on the sandy kitchen floor.

'Don't worry,' said Zmyrna. 'Always little bit spills. Domina calls it libation to gods.'

Threptus watched as she eased the amphora back up against the wall and let the pointed end settle into the cone-shaped depression in the floor. Then she carefully replaced the big cork.

'Have you seen the evil spirit?' he asked her.

Zmyrna gazed at the ground and nodded.

Threptus swallowed. 'What does it look like?'

Slowly, Zmyrna raised her right hand and clenched it. 'It has eye as big as this,' she whispered, pointing to her fist. 'Is most terrible thing I ever see.'

Threptus was so surprised he almost dropped

the garum bottle. Instead he made the sign against evil and spat on the sandy floor.

Zmyrna lifted her gaze. 'I pray so hard your master rids us of this thing.'

'He will,' said Threptus with as much confidence as he could muster. But when they returned to the study he wasn't sure. Floridius was helping himself to a second goblet of wine. Threptus had quickly learned that when his master drank too much neat wine, he usually slept hard.

They had started dinner early, but the sun was already sinking behind the low roof. It was November, and the hours of day were shorter than the hours of night. As soon as the sun disappeared, the air grew chilly.

Zmyrna brought in a platter of grapes for dessert. They were big and black and bursting with sweetness.

'Before you retire to your cubiculum,' said Floridius through a mouthful of grapes. 'Do you have any black beans?'

'Only dried ones,' said Allia. 'How many do you need?'

'Just a handful. And some of those bronze

pans I saw. We'll need them, too.'

Allia herself brought two bronze saucepans, a medium sized one and a small one full of dried black beans. She put them on the table along with a sharp carving knife.

'I thought this might come in handy, too,' she said.

'Thank you,' said Floridius, barely glancing at the table. He had dragged the leather armchair out into the walkway and was settling himself in it. 'Do you have any spare blankets?' he added.

'Of course,' said Allia, and to Zmyrna. 'Bring two blankets from the cedarwood chest.'

She narrowed her eyes at Floridius. 'You won't be too comfortable there, will you? You won't fall asleep?'

'We won't sleep a wink,' proclaimed Floridius. 'From here we can see the garden and all three doorways.'

'Four,' said Threptus, bringing one of the wooden chairs out so that he could sit beside his mentor. 'We can see the front door, too.'

'Very well,' said Allia. 'I have lit two hanging oil-lamps. They should burn until dawn. If you get thirsty, there is that big dolium of water in the kitchen.'

'At midnight I must perform a rite,' said Floridius, 'so do not be alarmed by the loud clashing of pans.'

'May Fortuna give you good luck,' said Allia. She handed them each a woollen blanket, a pale blue one for Threptus and an orange-and-red striped one for Floridius. 'We are going to use the latrine and then go to bed. Goodnight.'

'Goodnight, domina,' said Floridius.

The two women went first to the kitchen, then into their bedroom.

Threptus heard the bolt slide across.

It was dusk now, and the sky over the garden was a vibrant blue, the colour of a peacock's feather. Threptus folded up his legs on the wooden chair and wrapped the soft blue blanket around his shoulders. After his long session in the sea, his skin felt clean and soft. He was warm and cozy, and for the first time in days his stomach was full.

From somewhere outside the house a blackbird gave its piercing warning cry. A cat yowled and the voice of Praeco the town crier came faintly: 'Day has ended; night begins. May Jupiter, Juno and Minerva preserve us!'

Threptus knew from long experience that unless there was a fire or some other emergency, Praeco would not cry the hour again until midnight.

That was when he and Floridius must perform the rite. Midnight.

Threptus felt a thrill of fear mixed with excitement. What form would the evil spirit take? Floridius said spirits looked like gauzy, white floating masks with gaping eyes. But Allia described something like a snake's shadow. Or would it be a goat-bearded, goat-horned demon, with an eye in its tummy the size of Zmyrna's fist? Threptus shivered.

Something else was puzzling him.

'What are you going to do with the black beans and the copper pans?' he asked Floridius, who was tucking his striped blanket around himself.

'At midnight we walk around the house scattering the beans over our right shoulders,' said Floridius with a yawn. 'That attracts the demons. Then we bang the pans to scare them away forever.'

'Do you think we'll have to use the knife?'

The only answer he received was a soft snore. Floridius was already fast asleep.

SCROLL XI

THREPTUS STARED OVER AT HIS sleeping mentor and smiled. He didn't mind keeping vigil alone. He would wake Floridius if he heard a noise.

In the meantime what could he do?

He could practise whistling so that next time the magistrate came, he would be able to warn Floridius.

Threptus made his mouth into an O and blew. Nothing.

He tried tightening the O.

He tried softening the O.

He tried blowing harder.

He tried blowing softer.

Finally he got it. It just happened. He was whistling!

And once he'd discovered how to do it, it was easy.

He whistled a little tune and then realised he was supposed to be listening for the larva or demon or whatever it was.

So he sat forward and listened.

He heard the rustle of some small animal in the shrubs, a dog barking in a house nearby, the distant hoot of an owl. All these sounds were familiar to him from when he used to sleep in the graveyard. Soon the moon would rise above the tiled roof.

Threptus's stomach was full and the blanket was soft. He would just close his eyes for a moment, to pray for his kitten Felix and the sacred chickens who were all alone at home. He hoped they weren't worried about him and wondering where he was . . .

Threptus woke with a start, his heart pounding. The garden was bathed in eerie moonlight, so that everything looked either black or silver. Great Juno's beard! He must have been asleep for hours! But something had woken him.

Threptus slipped off the chair, letting his blanket drop away. A few steps took him into the small garden. He looked up. The full moon was almost directly overhead. That meant it was nearly midnight.

Threptus heard a dog bark somewhere far away.

That was not what had woken him.

He heard an owl hoot, nearby.

That was not what had woken him.

Then he heard a strange liquid plop from near the myrrh tree.

That was the sound that had woken him.

Carefully, cautiously, Threptus crept forward. In the eerie light of the moon, the twisted tree looked evil. It seemed to reach its thorny branches towards him.

Plop!

There it was again. A soft splashing sound.

It must be coming from the well at the foot of the spooky myrrh tree.

Threptus's knees were shaking so much that he could hardly stand, but he remembered Lupus. 'Be brave,' he told himself. 'Be brave.'

He clutched the glass eye amulet around his neck with his right hand and made the sign against evil with his left.

He forced himself to take another step. And another.

Finally he reached the well. Slowly he leaned forward to look down into it.

He heard another plop and then he saw something he could scarcely believe.

In the black water of the well – lit by the ghastly light of the full moon – was a demonic eye the size of Zmyrna's fist.

The eye was looking straight back up at him.

SCROLL XII

THE GIANT EYE STARED UP AT THREPTUS from the inky water in the well.

'Ahhhhh!' Threptus screamed and jumped back so quickly that he fell over a shrub and knocked the air out of his lungs. When his breath returned he scrambled to his feet, turned and ran towards Floridius: 'AGGHHHHH!'

'Chickens!' cried Floridius, jolted out of

a dream, and then, 'Where am I? What's happened?'

'The evil eye!' Threptus tugged his mentor's blanket so hard that it fell onto the floor. 'There's a demon in the well and it gave me the evil eye!'

'Really?' Floridius looked surprised.

'Yes! It was horrible!' Threptus's voice was shaking and his heart was pounding. For a moment he thought he might be sick.

Floridius heaved himself out of the leather chair. 'Are you sure?' he said. 'A giant eye in the well?'

'Yes!' Threptus caught his hand and pulled. 'Come on!' he said.

Floridius was reluctant to enter the garden, so Threptus had to get behind him and push. Gradually he urged his mentor towards the well. Floridius was moving slowly, holding up his left hand palm forward and spitting with every step.

Finally they reached the well. Threptus could not bear to look down a second time at the horrible thing so he covered his eyes with his fingers and hung back, waiting for his master to scream in terror.

Floridius hesitantly leaned over the well, looked down and laughed. 'Ha, ha!'

'What?' said Threptus, peeking through his fingers.

'Have another look!' Floridius was obviously relieved.

Threptus took a few tentative steps towards the well and took a very quick peek. Then he looked again. The inky surface of the water showed only a trembling silver moon.

'Silly boy!' chuckled Floridius, and ruffled Threptus's hair. 'It's just a reflection of the moon. You had me quite convinced.'

'That's not what I saw!' cried Threptus. 'I saw a giant evil eye. It looked right at me. Now I'm going to die of pooing and vomiting.'

Floridius patted him on the head. 'Don't worry, me little friend,' he said. 'Once we perform the ritual you'll be fine. Come help me scatter the beans?'

Threptus nodded vigorously and followed Floridius back to the lamplit study where the brass pans waited. His teeth were chattering.

Floridius poured the dried beans into a fold of his toga.

He went to the altar and put a few beans on it.

Then he intoned: 'O lemures, larvae and/or demons! Feed on these beans and be satisfied. Come and feed.' He tossed a few beans over his right shoulder. 'Don't look behind you,' he said to Threptus. 'Stay close to me and look at the ground.'

Floridius moved out of the study and along the portico. Threptus stayed close. He could hear the rattle of black beans falling on the walkway.

'Now turn your back to the garden,' said Floridius. Threptus and his mentor both faced the kitchen. Floridius tossed the remaining beans over his shoulder. Threptus heard them patter onto the leaves of garden shrubs.

'Now,' said Floridius to Threptus. 'Do you want to bang the pans together? Or shall I?'

In his excitement, Threptus made a rude noise with his bottom.

'Great Juno's beard!' chuckled Floridius. 'That might keep away the demons. But banging the pans is more effective.'

'Don't bang them yet,' cried Threptus, running into the kitchen. 'I need the latrine!'

He got there just in time. He lifted his tunic and sat on the polished board with its hole.

Ahhh! That was better.

As Threptus leaned forward to reach for the sponge-stick in its beaker of vinegar, he felt something touch his bottom from underneath. It was cold and wet and rubbery and *alive*.

'AGGHHHHH!' he cried.

He found himself at least six feet from the latrine, near the wide kitchen door. Floridius came running in, brandishing the carving knife.

'What?' he cried. 'What is it?'

Threptus was too horrified to speak. He could only point.

Rising up from the hole in the polished board, like a cobra from a basket, was something like the thick tendril of a grey vine. At first Threptus thought it was a snake. Then he saw the suckers and he realised what it was.

It was a tentacle.

The tentacle of a giant octopus.

'See? I told you I wasn't imagining it.' Threptus looked at Floridius just in time to see his mentor's eyes roll back into his head.

Thud!

Floridius had fainted and collapsed on the floor like a sack of beans.

Threptus looked back at the giant tentacle.

It groped here and there, lightly touched the pots and amphoras ranged along the right-hand wall of the kitchen. It seemed to be looking for something. Then it found the patch of fish sauce on the sandy floor. It moved along a series of drops to the work-table, where Zmyrna had left the glass bottle. When the tentacle touched the glass bottle of garum, it seemed to find what it had been looking for.

For a split second it paused.

Then – with one swift motion – the tentacle slithered back into the toilet, taking the bottle of fish sauce with it.

'OH DEAR,' MURMURED FLORIDIUS as he came to. 'Oh dear, oh dear. What happened?'

Threptus stopped splashing him with water from the big jug and helped him sit up.

'A giant octopus,' he said. 'It wasn't a demon. It was a giant octopus.'

'How?' said Floridius.

'I've been thinking about that,' said Threptus. 'I think the main sewer goes right underneath this house. Under the well and the latrine. The river's nearby, isn't it? So things could come up the sewer as well as go out into it, couldn't they?'

'I suppose you're right' said Floridius, as Threptus helped him to his feet. 'There's an outlet in the river bank not far from here. I fish there sometimes and I've seen water gushing out. That would explain how that octopus got here and how it could appear in the well and also in the latrine.' He gave a shudder of disgust.

'And that's why the water in the well smells bad,' said Threptus. 'It's sewer water, not well water.'

'What on earth do you think it wanted?' Floridius nervously eyed the small latrine and made the sign against evil.

'It wanted garum.'

'Why garum?' said Floridius.

Threptus shrugged. 'Because it's so tasty?'

'You know that garum is made out of the fermented blood and guts of fish?'

'It is?' said Threptus. He pondered this for a moment. Then shrugged.

'That octopus is used to eating fish,' said Floridius, 'And garum is the closest thing to it in this house.'

'Also it's tasty,' said Threptus, and added, 'What if the octopus comes back?'

'Let's make sure it doesn't,' said Floridius. Go get those bronze saucepans. We'll make a noise so loud that it will swim away and never ever return.'

Threptus ran to the study to get the pans.

When he got back, he stood over the small latrine and banged the two copper saucepans as hard as he could.

The noise was horrendous.

Floridius stuck his chubby fingers in his ears.

Threptus grinned; he liked the noise. He banged the pans even harder.

After some time, he caught sight of Allia Porra and Zmyrna standing in the open kitchen door. Both had blankets wrapped around their shoulders and their fingers in their ears.

Threptus stopped banging. When his ears stopped ringing, he heard watchdogs barking all over town. Soon the whole port of Ostia would be awake.

'What is it?' cried Allia. 'Did you find the spirit?'

'Yes,' said Floridius. 'We found it all right.'

'It was a giant oct—' began Threptus, but Floridius clapped a hand over his mouth.

'It was a giant sewer demon!' lisped the soothsayer. 'Most horrible thing I've ever seen.'

'What did it want?' cried Allia.

'Your gar—' began Threptus. But once again, Floridius stopped him from speaking.

'Your lives!' he cried. 'It wanted your lives.'

'Oh!' cried the two women. They both made the sign against evil, spat and then clutched each other in pure terror.

'But do not fear!' declared Floridius. 'I have vanquished it once and for all.'

'Are you certain?'

'I am certain. You can go back to bed now. You won't be disturbed again.'

But his proclamation was immediately proved false when a pounding on the door brought their heads round and they all heard a cry of 'Open up in the name of the duumvir, Marcus Artorius Bato!'

'POLLUX!' CURSED FLORIDIUS UNDER his breath. 'What's *he* doing here?'

'I open, domina,' said Zmyrna, but they all three followed her across the gravel path, silver in the moonlit garden.

Zmyrna opened the door to reveal the torchlit duumvir. Marcus Artorius Bato stood glaring, with his hands on his hips. To his right stood the lictor and a torch-bearing slave hovered behind them.

'You!' cried Bato, glaring at Floridius. 'Haven't you given me enough trouble today? Now you've made enough noise to wake the dead in their graves.'

Everyone made the sign against evil and spat.

'Allia Porra,' said Floridius. 'Allow me to present Marcus Artorius Bato, Ostia's recently elected duumvir.'

'I'm sorry about the noise,' said Allia. 'Floridius here was ridding the house of an evil sewer demon.'

'A likely story,' said Bato coldly. 'This man is a trickster and a fraud.'

'I am not!' cried Floridius. 'I am a bona fide soothsayer. In fact . . .' here he paused and his eyes rolled back into his head. 'I'm getting . . .'
For a moment Threptus thought his mentor was going to faint again. But no. Floridius was apparently having a prophetic moment.

'I'm getting something for you, Marcus Artorius Bato!'

Bato glanced nervously at his lictor. 'Don't be ridiculous.'

Floridius rolled his head and moaned: 'Hmmm. Ummm. Bummm.' Then he opened his eyes. 'Cheese!' he declared. 'Beware cheese!'

'What?' cried Bato.

'Beware cheese. It is not good for you.'

The lictor stifled a smile. 'He's right about that,' he said to Bato under his breath.

'And cumin-dusted eggs!' cried Floridius. 'The goddess Fortuna says cumin-dusted eggs will always be . . . unfortunate.'

Behind Bato, the torch-bearing slave nodded vigorously and flapped his hand in front of his nose, as if waving away a bad smell.

Threptus stared hard at the ground. At this point, bursting into laughter would not be helpful.

Floridius rolled his head and moaned: 'Hmmm. Ummm. Bummm.'

Bato opened his mouth to say something but Floridius got in first. 'But Fortuna says there is something that will be good for you.'

Bato's eyes narrowed. 'What does the goddess Fortuna advise?'

'I'm getting a name . . .' said Floridius. 'Lucilia! Yes, Lucilia.'

Even in the flickering torchlight, Threptus saw that Bato's face had grown pale. The duumvir rounded on his lictor. 'Whom did you tell?'

'Nobody, sir!' cried Bacillus. He looked genuinely shocked.

Bato turned back to Floridius. 'How do you know about Lucilia?'

'Fortuna!' said Floridius. 'She speaks to me sometimes. She promises an auspicious pairing with this Lucilia. I see fame, fortune and . . .' Floridius closed his eyes for a moment and announced: 'Babies!'

'Babies?' said Bato.

'Babies,' said Floridius. 'Heirs to your talent, beauty and greatness. Fine young sons. At least three of them.'

'Hmmph!' said Bato. But Threptus could see he was pleased.

'Now will you give me a licence to practise the art of prophesy in the forum?' said Floridius.

Bato glanced at his lictor.

'He did know about the cheese and the eggs, boss,' said Bacillus. 'And I haven't told a soul what you told me about Lucilia.'

Bato narrowed his eyes at Floridius. 'Does Fortuna tell you whether Lucilia and her father will accept my proposal of marriage?'

'Fortuna says . . . Hmmm . . . Ummm . . . Bummm . . . Fortuna says YES!' cried Floridius. And added with a wink, 'How could anyone refuse someone as handsome and powerful as you, O Bato?'

'Very well,' said Bato. 'I will give you a provisional licence to utter your prophecies in the forum. But if Lucilia Gamala turns me down then I'll revoke it.'

'Deal!' beamed Floridius, and stuck out his hand.

Bato curled his lip and said, 'Don't push your luck, Floridius. I'll be watching you. Come, Bacillus. Come, Fax, let's go home and try to get some sleep.'

'One more thing, duumvir?' said Floridius.

Bato turned back.

'Beneath this house runs a sewer connected to the Tiber. Correct?'

'That's true,' said Bato. When I was a junior magistrate I was in charge of sewer maintenance.

The sewer empties into the river not far from here. Why do you ask?'

'I ask because the demon came up via the sewer. Unless you want more sightings of this demon, I suggest you put bars over the place where the sewer empties into the Tiber.'

Bato raised an eyebrow, then nodded. 'Very well.' He turned to his lictor. 'Remind me to do that first thing in the morning.'

As soon as Zmyrna closed the door Floridius did a little dance. 'Oh ho, ho!' he chuckled. 'I'm official!' He ruffled Threptus's hair. 'We're in business.'

'Do you mean to say you were practising without a licence?' asked Allia Porra, looking down her long nose at him.

'Only a little,' said Floridius with a sheepish grin. 'And besides, demons don't care whether you're official or not. The only people who care about that are magistrates.'

Allia stifled a smile. 'True,' she admitted. 'But how can you ensure the demon stays away from my house?'

'Well, domina, we've driven it off for tonight

and Bato has promised to put bars on the entrance. But you know what politicians are like. Ha, ha!'

Allia was not amused. 'Just tell me what to do.' They were walking back towards the study.

Floridius gestured at the well as they passed by. 'I suggest you cover your well, for one thing, and your latrine pit too. I know a man who can do that for you. Petrus the stonemason. Just tell him I sent you. Five sesterces finder's fee. Plus the fifty for our vigil tonight. Plus ten for your two amulets. Only I'll give you those two for the price of one.'

'And we don't need to do anything else?' said Allia Porra. She went to a shelf in the study and brought a small cash box to the table. She removed a ring from her finger and Threptus saw that it had the teeth of a key in it. Using the key ring, Allia opened the box.

Floridius's eyes widened when he saw the gold coins inside. 'If you wanted to be extra safe,' he said, 'you could hang a few of me glass eyes from that tree in the middle of your garden. They're one sestertius each, but I'll give you two for the price of one, like I did for your amulets.'

Zmyrna whispered something in Allia's ear.

'How,' said Allia, 'will we relieve ourselves if the latrine is blocked up?'

'Use a chamber pot, like we do. I can sell you a nice one,' said Floridius. He winked at Threptus and they said together, 'Only five sesterces.'

*

Later that morning, Threptus and Floridius sat at a small folding table in the soothsayer's front yard. They had just enjoyed a breakfast of fresh honey cakes, still warm from Pistor's ovens. At their feet pecked fifteen happy chickens, for Threptus and his mentor had scattered the honey-soaked crumbs freely. Felix the grey kitten sat on Threptus's lap, purring loudly; his little belly was full of warm milk.

Now Threptus held a quill pen in his hand and was dipping it in a small clay saucer of ink. As Floridius watched, Threptus carefully formed three letters, and with hardly a smudge, he finished the letter:

From Threptus in the port of Ostia to Lupus in the port of Ephesus:

Greetings! Yesterday I went down into the sewers and you would be amazed. Then last night I solved the mystery of the demon in the latrines. It turned out to be a giant octopus that loved garum. It was terrorising a widow and her slave-girl, but now it will not bother them any more. The widow was very happy that we scared it away and she paid Floridius L sesterces, as agreed. She promised to block up a well in the garden, and also their latrine, but in the meantime she bought our whole stock of blue-and-white glass eyes. Floridius gave her two for the price of one and she hung up all XXX from a small thorny tree in the middle of her garden. You should see the tree. It looks as if it has eyes instead of leaves. That should keep away any evil spirits as well as the octopus! For one night's work we got LXXX sesterces because there was also the finder's fee of V sesterces for Petrus the stonemason.

Here is the tally:

* Doing the vigil = L
* Two Medusa amulets for the price of one = V
* Finder's fee for Petrus = V
* A chamber pot = V
* XXX glass eye amulets (two for the price of one) = XV

That adds up to LXXX. I can't even count that high. Floridius says that's as many as all the fingers and toes on IV people! He gave me II sesterces for helping him.

Also, do you remember the magistrate called Bato? He is going to give Floridius a licence to be an official soothsayer in the forum (as long as a woman named Lucilia Gamala agrees to marry him). That means Floridius will be able to help lots more people, and I can help him help them! So you can see that I am carrying on your good work as you asked me to do the day you left Ostia. I am also learning to read and write. My mentor Floridius has written this letter for me, but I dictated it. And now with my own hand I bid you, VALE!